A Collection of Wonderful Stories
for 7 year old Boys:

1 am a 7 year old super boy

(Inspirational Gift Books for Kids)

Table of Contents

Welcome to Your Own World of Magic!

Dear boy,

You are about to embark on an amazing adventure, a journey through many magical and inspiring stories. Each tale in this book is a treasure chest, waiting for you to unlock its secrets and discover the wonders inside.

As you turn these pages, you'll meet characters like Alex, who found himself in a world of his own making and almost disappeared into a black hole. You'll adventure with Tommy, who will have to choose between a mountain of candy and a little kindness and perseverance.

There's Charlie, the hardworking son of Mr. Harrington, who will understand the true value of what our elders leave behind. You'll meet Clever Pirate Tom, who sailed the seven seas and found the greatest treasure of all.

Each story is a journey, and the hero is [insert drumroll here!]...YOU! Yes, that's right! Like these wonderful characters, you have within you the strength, courage, and heart to overcome challenges and make your dreams come true.

Remember, every page turned is a step on the path of discovery. The adventures, the mysteries, the challenges, and the victories – all are parts of the journey that will help you understand the world around you and the strength that lives inside you, the magic that only you possess.

So, open this book with an eager heart and a curious mind. Let these stories be your guide and inspiration. Dream big, believe in yourself, and always know that the power is inside you, and if you can dream it, you can do it.

Welcome to your great adventure!

Timmy and Mondo's Nighttime Adventures

In a snug house on Maple Street lived a young boy named Timmy. One night there was a terrible storm, and all the lights in the house went out. The howling wind, rattling windows, and strange shadows frightened

Timmy, making him believe that when his room was dark, all the unknown monsters from his storybooks were all around him. Since that night, Timmy always slept with a comforting night light by his bed.

However, Timmy's parents thought he was growing up and should start to overcome his fear. They decided it was time for him to sleep without the night light. The first night without it, Timmy felt brave, but his room looked so different in the dark. The familiar corners and furniture seemed to turn into shadowy figures, and the silence of the night was filled with unknown whispers.

To feel a little safer, Timmy decided to grab his flashlight from the wardrobe for comfort. But to his astonishment, when he opened the wardrobe, he found a colorful, goofy monster with wiggly tentacles and big, twinkling eyes! The monster, just as surprised to see Timmy, began to cry big, colorful tears.

Forgetting his own fear, Timmy comforted the monster. "Hey, it's okay, don't cry," he said kindly. The monster sniffled and introduced himself as Mondo. Mondo lived in the wardrobe and was scared of Timmy because he had never seen a real boy before! They both laughed, realizing their fears were quite similar.

Timmy and Mondo spent the whole night talking and sharing stories. Mondo told Timmy about his monster world, while Timmy shared his own experiences. They soon began to create fantastic adventures right there in Timmy's room. With blankets as their magic carpets and pillows as

mountains, every night, they embarked on imaginary journeys to distant lands.

Timmy's parents noticed him chatting and giggling to himself in his room at night. When Timmy told them about Mondo, they were puzzled but happy to see him less afraid of the dark.

With each passing night, Timmy's room transformed into a magical realm of adventure and friendship. He learned that the unknown isn't as scary once you get to know it. Darkness, which once frightened him, now held a world of wonder and excitement.

Thanks to Mondo, Timmy discovered that friendship could turn fear into fun, and even a wardrobe monster could become a best friend. Each night was filled with

laughter, friendship, and boundless imagination, making his room the most magical place in the world.

The Shiest Butterfly

In the deepest, most colorful part of the
jungle, where flowers bloomed in every hue
and the air was filled with the songs of
birds, there lived a shy butterfly named
Benny. Benny, with his soft, whispery voice
and delicate wings, often fluttered alone. He

longed to make friends but was too timid, watching other insects play from afar.

One sunny morning, Benny tried to land on a slippery, shiny flower. But, oh no! His wings got tangled in a twisty vine nearby. He wriggled and twisted, trying to free himself, but the vine held tight. Feeling a bit embarrassed and needing help, Benny called out to the nearby birds and bugs. Most of them were too busy, but then, a kind little ladybug named Lucy saw him.

Lucy flew over and gently helped untangle Benny's wings. Benny felt a rush of thankfulness but was too shy to say much. He fluttered off quickly, later feeling sorry for missing the chance to befriend Lucy.

Why had Lucy helped him? Benny was so shy that he spent most of his time on his

own. He had never imagined that all these creatures that seemed so different sometimes, so sure of themselves, laughing and working among friends, could be so generous and kind.

Since that day, Lucy started saying hello every time Benny flew by. But he always felt like the other bugs and birds looked at him with mistrust. When he heard laughter behind his back, he felt they were laughing at him. So, he still kept his distance, longing for the friendship and the fun everyone seemed to be having, except for him.

One day, while Benny was resting under a leaf, he noticed a commotion in the jungle. All the creatures seemed worried and were rushing about. Peeking out, Benny saw something scary – a large, menacing bird was chasing after Lucy!

Benny was terrified. The bird was huge, and its beak looked as sharp as a shark's tooth. He was paralyzed. But then he remembered how Lucy had helped him, and he sprang into action. He summoned all his courage, took a deep breath, and zoomed out from his hiding spot. He couldn't fight the bird; it was just too big and scary! So, he had an idea: with his wings shimmering in the sunlight, he created a dazzling whirl of colors. The light confused the big bird, and he became disoriented.

Taking advantage of the moment, Benny swooped down, scooped up Lucy, and darted back to the safety of the leaves. The big bird, still dazed by the blinding light, decided it was too much trouble and flew off.

When they were safe, all the jungle creatures who had been watching cheered for Benny. Lucy told everyone how brave Benny had been. The other bugs and birds realized that Benny wasn't just shy and quiet – he was also brave and kind.

From that day, Benny wasn't the shy butterfly anymore. He became a beloved hero in the jungle. All the creatures wanted to be friends with him, and they discovered that he had not only courage but also a big heart.

Dear reader, remember Benny's story. It shows us that when we help others and face our fears, we discover our own strength and bravery. Like Benny, you too can transform fear into friendship and loneliness into laughter. It's all about being kind, brave, and believing in yourself – becoming the superhero in your own story!

Max and the Magic Chair

Once, there was a boy named Max who loved having lots of friends. He often bragged about how many friends he had at school and how everyone liked him.

One day, his grandpa said to him, "Max, I'll bet you a big bag of your favorite candy that you don't have as many real friends as you think. Some might just be playmates or classmates, not true friends."

Max took the bet without a second thought. But he wasn't sure how to find out who his real friends were, so he asked his grandpa. His grandpa smiled and said, "I have just the thing you need. It's in the attic. Wait here."

Grandpa came back pretending to carry something invisible in his hand. "Here, take this. It's a magic chair. It's invisible and tricky to sit on, but if you take it to school and manage to sit on it, it will show you who your real friends are."

Max, curious and excited, took the invisible chair to school. During recess, he asked everyone to make a circle around him and announced, "Watch something amazing!"

As Max tried to sit on the invisible chair, he couldn't see it and fell down. Everyone laughed. Max didn't give up. He tried again and again, falling each time, which made everyone laugh more. But then, suddenly, when he tried once more, he didn't fall. He was sitting in mid-air!

Max looked around and saw his friends Sarah, Leo, and Emma holding him up so he wouldn't fall. The others, who he thought were his friends, had only laughed at him. Max realized then what his grandpa meant.

16

The show ended, and Max left with his three true friends. He told them about his grandpa's clever way of showing that real friends are those who care for us and will protect us from harm rather than just laughing when we fall or make a mistake.

That evening, the four friends went to see Max's grandpa, who was happy to pay the candy bet. They listened to his stories and ate candy (the kind that's really good but also pretty healthy!) until they couldn't eat anymore. And from then on, they used the magic chair test to find out who their true friends were. Many, many years later, the people who had caught them when they were about to fall were still their best friends. And when they grew up, got jobs, and got married, their children were also best friends with their friends' children.

Thanks to Grandpa's magic chair, Max learned a big lesson: having very good friends is much more important than having many friends.

Alex's Big Match

Once upon a sunny Saturday, a lively group of kids from the neighborhood gathered with an exciting plan: to organize their own soccer match, just like the ones they watched on TV. Each boy and girl was buzzing with anticipation, promising to bring something special to make the match feel professional. Alex was in charge of the ball, Ben would bring a shiny whistle, Ella had the goalposts, and so on. They even had goalkeeper gloves and bright corner flags!

As they met on the green field, the air was filled with the sounds of laughter and chatter. But excitement soon turned into a debate. Before they could start, they argued about who brought the most important item for the game. "Surely, the ball is most important," said Alex. "No, what's a game without goalposts?" argued Ella.

Unable to decide, they came up with a plan. They would start the game with all the items and then, one by one, remove each item to see which ones were truly essential.

The game began with a burst of energy. But soon, they ditched the whistle, with Ben shouting decisions instead. The game continued, still fun and lively. Next, the goalkeeper gloves were tossed aside. Surprisingly, the goals were saved just as well without them.

The corner flags were next to go, hardly missed in the excitement of the game. Even the goalposts were replaced with two large trash bins, which worked just fine. The children laughed and cheered, thoroughly enjoying themselves.

But then, they took it one step further and replaced the soccer ball with an old, dented tin can. The game carried on, but the tin can wobbled and bounced unpredictably, making their skilled kicks and passes go awry.

Just then, a woman and her young son strolled by the field. The woman, watching the game, commented to her son, "Look there, even without a real ball, those kids are managing to play. But they won't really improve their skills this way."

The kids overheard this and suddenly paused, realizing their game had strayed far from what they had imagined. Their fun match had turned into a chaotic display of pride and ego, losing the essence of a true soccer game.

In that moment of realization, the children decided to put their disagreements aside. They gathered the proper equipment, setting up the goalposts, fetching the ball, and even placing the corner flags back in their spots. They restarted the match, this time focusing not on who was the best or who brought the most important item but on playing together, improving their skills, and, most importantly, enjoying the game.

As they played, their laughter and cheers echoed across the field. They passed the ball with skill and precision, celebrated each goal with joy, and even when they missed, they encouraged each other. It was no longer about winning or showing off but about the thrill of the game and the bond of friendship.

And so, under the golden sun, the kids played the greatest soccer match of their lives. In the end, they saw that they didn't need a ball, goalposts, or gloves to play. All it really takes to have fun playing a game is to have a friend. You don't need fancy equipment or expensive toys.

The only truly essential thing the kids learned was to have each other.

The Superkid and the Greatest Power

In a land of amazing superkids, there was a big problem: the neighboring galaxy, Tlon, needed help to fight a league of villains. But the superkids couldn't agree on who should go.

"The best superkid needs X-ray vision to see through walls and surprise the bad guys," said the kids with X-ray eyes.

"No, you need super-speed to catch them!" argued the super-fast kids.

"But they always fly away. You have to fly to be the best," said the flying kids.

"Our super strength is the most important," declared the super-strong kids.

They argued and argued until a super-smart kid showed up with an ordinary-looking friend. He was small, skinny, and didn't even have a superhero costume.

"This is Jake, and he will solve our problem," said the super-smart kid confidently.

Everyone was shocked. "What? How? Does he have secret powers? Can he fight the bad guys?" they asked, puzzled.

"I don't know Jake's secret, but he's amazing," replied the super-smart kid.

At first, everyone thought it was a joke. But as they couldn't agree on who should go, and they trusted the super-smart kid to make the best decision, they all agreed to send the ordinary kid to the galaxy of Tlon.

The ordinary kid called Jake traveled for many light years until he finally made it to Tlon, the galaxy that was in trouble. When he arrived, everyone was surprised. They had sent a superkid with no powers?

Weeks passed, and Jake didn't catch a single bad guy. But somehow, the galaxy of Tlon seemed more at peace. When it was time to send Jake home, so many people came to say goodbye that the galaxy's leaders got curious. They found out that the jails were almost empty, and there was hardly any crime anymore!

When Jake got back home, news of his success spread fast. The bad guys, the League of Incorrigible Villains, didn't want the same thing that had happened in Tlon to happen in their galaxy. So, they kidnapped Jake to discover his superpower. "I don't have powers," the kid said. "I just try to make people happy. I help, share, forgive, smile..."

While talking with the villains, Jake juggled, gave out sweets and hugs, told jokes, and helped everyone. The bad guys felt so happy and relaxed that they forgot about doing bad things and breaking laws.

And that's how an ordinary kid changed the whole wide Universe without catching a single villain! His kindness made everyone feel so good that they didn't want to be evil anymore. His secret was so powerful that the other superkids imitated him; they stopped using their own superpowers to adopt this special one.

That's why kids like you don't have superpowers like flying or super-speed today. You have the most important power of all: the power to brighten someone's day. Use it well – the Universe needs you!

Prince Charlie and the Year of Magical Toys

Once upon a time in a faraway kingdom, there lived a little 7-year-old prince named Charlie. Charlie lived in a grand castle with towering spires and had everything a boy could ever wish for. But he was so spoiled that he made a peculiar rule: if someone gave a toy to any child in the kingdom, they had to buy an extra one for him. As a result, Charlie's playroom was overflowing with every toy imaginable.

One sunny day, a mysterious toymaker known for creating the most wondrous and whimsical toys arrived in the kingdom. Prince Charlie was fascinated by these unique toys and eagerly invited the toymaker to live in the castle for a year. He promised the toymaker a chest full of gold and jewels if he made a new toy for Charlie every day. The toymaker, with a twinkle in his eye, agreed but set one important condition: "My toys are special and need care. You must play with each one every day. Can you do that?"

Charlie, eyes gleaming with excitement, agreed without hesitation.

Thus, every morning, as the sun rose over the kingdom, Charlie found a new, more marvelous toy waiting for him. A wind-up dragon that breathed real smoke, a tiny circus with acrobats that flipped and twirled, a magical train that chugged around the room – the toys were like nothing Charlie had ever seen.

But as days turned into weeks, Charlie's collection grew so large that it was impossible to play with all of them. So, he started to skip some, hoping the toymaker wouldn't notice. But the toymaker's toys were magical, and they didn't like being ignored.

One night, as Charlie snuggled into his royal bed, the unused toys came to life. They marched in a line, demanding their playtime. The little prince, rubbing his sleepy eyes, had to stay up late, playing with each neglected toy.

The next day, Charlie was so tired he overslept and had less time to play. He met the new toy, a laughing jester that juggled sparkling balls but then had to rush through playing with the others. He was exhausted and hardly enjoyed his playtime.

Days passed, and each was worse than the last. Charlie was running from toy to toy, playing while eating, talking, and even bathing. His royal life had turned into a whirlwind of toys and tiredness.

One gloomy afternoon, as Charlie gazed out of his window, he saw a group of village children playing joyfully with a simple stone. An idea sparked in his weary mind. He called the children to the castle. They arrived, their faces clouded with worry, fearing the prince would take their stone.

But Charlie surprised them. He didn't want the stone; he wanted to play with them and share his toys. The children's eyes widened with delight as they played with the magical toys. When they were done, Charlie did something he had never done before – he let each child take home their favorite toy.

Charlie's plan was a success! He had fewer toys, which meant more fun and less stress. Plus, he made new friends. Each day, he invited more children to the castle, sharing his toys and having a royal good time!

When the year was up, and it was time for the toymaker to leave, all 365 magical toys had found new homes with children across the kingdom. The once lonely and overwhelming playroom in the castle had transformed into the most joyous playroom in all the land.

Prince Charlie had learned a valuable lesson: sharing brings more happiness than having everything to yourself. With his new friends, he shared adventures worth more than all the toys in the world.

Sam and the Ring of Trouble

Once upon a time, there was a 7-year-old boy named Sam who loved to explore. One day, while playing in the park, Sam spotted a shiny ring on the ground. It belonged to his neighbor, Mr. Thompson, who was getting ready for a very special anniversary celebration with his wife. Mr. Thompson had accidentally left the ring outside, and Sam, overcome with curiosity, decided to try it on quickly. But when he tried to take it off, it got stuck on his finger!

"Oh no! I'm going to get caught. I need to think of something fast!" Sam thought to himself. He quickly left the park, hoping to figure out a way to remove the ring later.

Mr. Thompson was really upset when he realized his ring was missing. He was known as the best problem-solver in the neighborhood, and soon, everyone was on the lookout for someone wearing a ring. Sam, hearing about the search, felt really embarrassed and scared. "I've got to hide this ring," he thought.

In a panic, Sam found a bucket of black paint where the anniversary party was being set up. He dipped his hand in it to cover the ring. As he ran away, paint dripped everywhere, spoiling the decorations and even splashing on Mrs. Thompson's dress!

When Mr. Thompson saw the mess, he was even more upset. Now he told everyone to forget about the ring and try to find someone with a hand covered in black paint. Sam was in trouble again! He wrapped his hand in bandages, pretending he had had an accident.

Sam thought he was safe until he ran into Mr. Thompson, who felt sorry for him and insisted on taking him to the hospital. Sam was worried because an X-ray would reveal the ring, and removing the bandage would show the paint.

Thinking quickly, Sam told Mr. Thompson he needed to stop by his house first. Once home, he cleverly wrapped his hand in heavy materials so the X-ray wouldn't show the ring. He then re-bandaged his hand with loads of glue, making it impossible to take off.

Feeling relieved, Sam left to meet Mr. Thompson, but he hadn't thought about how hard it would be to move his hand with the heavy wrapping. As he tried to walk, he tripped and fell right on top of Mr. Thompson!

Soon, ambulances and neighbors rushed over. They found the bandages, the heavy wrapping, the paint, and the ring. Everyone thought Sam had planned to spoil the anniversary celebration. He quickly became the most misunderstood boy in the neighborhood and felt really sad.

After some time, Mr. Thompson talked to Sam, who tearfully explained everything: he hadn't meant to ruin the party; he just was too embarrassed to admit his mistake.

Sam learned a big lesson that day. He realized that one small mistake and trying to cover it up could lead to a lot of trouble.

Mr. Thompson, seeing that Sam had learned his lesson, forgave him and helped him explain everything to the neighbors. Sam's story taught everyone that telling the truth is always better than making up stories to cover up little mistakes. And from that day, Sam became known as the most honest kid in the neighborhood.

Max and the Shrinking World

Once upon a time, in a land very far away where secrets hid in every corner, there was a very naughty villain named Max the Mischief-Maker. Max wasn't just your average troublemaker; he was the sneakiest and smartest of them all. He lived in a big castle with lots of secret passages and rooms, where he came up with all sorts of tricky ideas and gadgets.

Max's latest scheme was his most ambitious yet. He wanted to turn the world into a dark, joyless place. He spent nights and days tinkering and inventing, creating a potion that made people too tired to do anything fun or important and a super stinky gas that was so smelly it made people want to hide away in their homes.

Slowly, the world started to change. Parks became empty, streets were silent, and laughter was rarely heard. But Max noticed something odd. Amidst the gloominess, there was a light that never faded – the strength and happiness of families.

No matter how small he made the houses with his shrinking ray, families found comfort in being close together. When he made their food disappear with his vanishing machine, families shared whatever crumbs they had, making the most of it with smiles and stories.

Max was baffled. He couldn't understand what made these families so resilient. He spied on them with his sneaky spy drones and finally discovered their secret. It was love that made families strong, and there was no machine or potion that could destroy it.

Determined to find a way to break this love, Max worked tirelessly. But no matter how many gadgets he built, he couldn't find a way to overcome the power of family love.

Feeling frustrated and defeated, Max turned off his machines and let the world return to its cheerful self. He was so downhearted that he didn't know where to turn. In his moment of sadness, he found himself walking to the only place he hadn't been in years, his parents' cozy little house.

Knocking timidly on the door, Max was engulfed in a warm embrace as soon as his parents saw him. He spilled out his heart, telling them about his failed plans and how he discovered the strength of family love. Despite everything he had done, his parents just held him tighter, forgave him, and encouraged him to use his talents for good.

Max's heart felt lighter than it had in years. He realized that even a villain like him had a family that loved and forgave him unconditionally. Inspired by this revelation,

Max decided to turn his life around. He transformed his fortress into a place of fun and invention for good, inviting families from all over to enjoy his new, friendly gadgets and toys.

And so, Max the Mischief-Maker became Max the Marvel-Maker, known far and wide not for his villainy but for his heart and his amazing inventions that brought joy to families everywhere. It just goes to show even the most mischievous among us can find redemption in the love of a family.

Tommy Buys a Little Happiness

Every month, young Tommy and his cousins eagerly awaited the family feast at Grandpa and Grandma's house, a cozy home filled with laughter and delicious smells. The highlight for the kids was always when Grandpa, with a twinkle in his eye, handed out a few shiny coins to each child, saying, "Go buy a little happiness!" Off they would scamper, pockets jingling, to the nearby candy store, where they'd choose from rows of colorful sweets, bubble gum, and jellybeans.

The grown-ups, watching this monthly ritual, often murmured that the kids needed to learn to manage money. So, one sunny afternoon, they proposed a year-long challenge: "Let's see what you can do with your coins over a whole year!"

The cousins' reactions varied. Sarah and Ben, the thoughtful ones, decided to save their coins in little piggy banks. However, Leo and Max, the youngest and most impulsive, couldn't resist the lure of sweets. They kept spending all their coins on candy, showing off their sugary treasures and giggling.

Annie, the entrepreneurial cousin, had a different plan. She started trading toys, making small bets in friendly card games, and soon amassed a neat little pile of coins. Her clever dealings became the talk of the family gatherings, but her luck didn't last. One risky bet on a toy car race wiped out all her savings.

Then there was Alex, whose determination was as solid as a rock. He saved every coin in a heavy, old-fashioned jar, dreaming of victory. Alex's patience paid off. At the end of the year, he had saved the most coins. With his savings, he struck a deal with the candy store owner for a bulk purchase of sweets at a discount. On the day of the challenge, Alex proudly displayed not just a mountain of sweets but also a shiny new toy car. He was the clear winner, showing everyone the fruits of patience and saving.

But what about Tommy? On the day of the challenge, Tommy stood with empty pockets, his face a mix of disappointment and hope. He had a brilliant plan but had spent his coins too soon. Despite the skeptical looks from his relatives, Tommy was not discouraged.

Determined, Tommy continued his plan into the next year. Then, at the following year's family feast, Tommy unveiled his grand surprise. He walked in with a gleaming violin and a wallet thicker than anyone expected. With eyes wide, the family listened as Tommy played a beautiful melody on the violin. The music filled the room, touching everyone's hearts.

Tommy then shared his story. He had used Grandpa's coins to pay a kind violinist in the park for lessons. The violinist, impressed by Tommy's passion and dedication, had taught him eagerly. Their duets in the park were so popular that the man decided to gift Tommy his very own violin.

Tommy's journey to becoming a talented violinist inspired everyone. His story wasn't just about saving coins; it was about investing in a dream. The family realized that Tommy's "little happiness" had grown into a lifelong passion, all thanks to a few coins and a lot of determination.

From that day, Tommy's violin melodies became a beloved part of the family feasts, and his story taught everyone the value of patience and determination.

If you really, really want something, dear reader, don't squander your gifts on things that will disappear as soon as candy melts in your mouth. The greatest joys in life are reserved for those who dream big and will patiently work to achieve their dreams.

Danny's Fantastic Virtual Turtles

Once, there was a 7-year-old boy named Danny who loved computers and video games more than anything. He could sit for hours playing his favorite game, where he guided a character through endless levels to collect turtles.

Danny was so good at it that he probably had more virtual turtles than anyone else in the world. Whenever his family urged him to take a break and join them, Danny would say, "But this is my doorway to the world. There's so much to discover here!"

One day, something unbelievable happened. When Danny turned on his computer after school, he heard a loud, cracking sound, like glass breaking. To his amazement, hundreds of little turtles, just like the ones from his game, started pouring out of his screen! They filled every corner of his room.

Danny couldn't believe his eyes. He restarted his computer and even called his parents to make sure he wasn't dreaming.

But the turtles were real, and they were here to stay.

His parents were shocked but decided that Danny should be responsible for the turtles. Looking after so many turtles was a big job. Danny learned everything about turtles – what they ate, how they lived – and he even tried to get them to leave his room, but they wouldn't budge.

Over time, Danny grew to love living with the turtles. He played with them, taught them tricks, and even gave them names. It was a lot of work, but it was also fun, and Danny loved to share his turtle adventures with his friends, family, and teachers.

One day, Danny realized he hadn't played his video game in a long time. He was too busy enjoying his real turtles and learning

about them. He was amazed to discover they could live a hundred years and hold their breath for seven hours! He started exploring nature outside, watching how turtles lived in the wild. Over time, he could tell when the turtles were hungry or sleepy by just looking at them, and he felt so happy they were a part of his life.

Then, just as suddenly as they appeared, the turtles vanished. His parents worried Danny might go back to his old, grumpy self, glued to his computer. But Danny didn't mind. He took his savings and ran to the pet shop. He came back with a real turtle and a tiny hedgehog to care for and learn about.

Today, Danny still loves learning about animals and nature. He uses his computer too, but now he mostly uses it for school and to learn more about his real-life pets.

Whenever someone asks about his hobbies, he points to his pets and says, "They're my real doorway to the world. There's so much more to them than you'd think!"

Little Leo and the Starry Night

Once upon a time, in a small, peaceful village nestled between rolling hills and lush forests lived a young boy named Leo. Leo was known for his curiosity and kindness, always eager to help his neighbors and explore the wonders of nature around him.

One clear, starry night, Leo noticed that the brightest star in the sky, which he always admired before going to bed, was flickering unusually. Intrigued, he decided to investigate. Packing a small bag with essentials and his trusty flashlight, Leo embarked on a nocturnal adventure.

As he trekked through the forest, guided by the star's light, Leo encountered various animals. He met a rabbit caught in a bush, a lost owl looking for its nest, and a family of beavers struggling to fix their dam. Although he was in a hurry to go look for his star, he didn't hesitate to help them. He disentangled the rabbit from the bush, helped the owl find his nest, and used some logs to fix the beavers' dam. Each time he helped, the star seemed to shine a little brighter.

Finally, Leo reached the top of a hill where the light from the star led him to a secret cave. Inside was a radiant crystal, shining brighter than any gem he had ever seen. The crystal spoke to him in a soft, melodic voice, revealing that it was the heart of the star, which was fading and had descended to find someone with a pure, loving heart to restore its power. Leo's acts of kindness had restored the crystal's energy.

The crystal granted Leo a wish for his good deeds. Leo wished for the happiness and well-being of all the villagers and the forest creatures. The crystal glowed brightly and fulfilled his wish, spreading joy and prosperity throughout the land.

Leo returned home, his heart full of joy. From that night on, the star shone brighter than ever, reminding everyone in the village of the power of kindness, generosity, and the magic that lies in selflessly helping others.

When you help someone, even when it is not the easiest thing to do, you are feeding the radiant heart of the world, which has the power to make all things bright, beautiful, and peaceful.

Tom Finds the Greatest Treasure

There once was a boy called Tommy, who didn't like school at all. He didn't enjoy studying or doing homework. One day, a famous pirate captain named Captain Stickybeard came to town looking for young adventurers to join his crew. Tommy, dreaming of treasure and adventure, was the first to sign up.

Aboard Captain Stickybeard's ship, life was all about hunting for treasure. The rule was strict: no reading or studying, or you'd be locked up with the hungry rats! Tommy thought this way of life sounded exciting, but being a pirate turned out to be tough. The crew scrubbed the deck, fixed the sails, and the treasure maps they found often led to small, disappointing treasures. They barely had enough money for food and clothes.

Captain Stickybeard always promised big treasures and sang songs about how great it was not to worry about reading or studying. But one day, Tommy's food was stolen. Starving, he sneaked into the dreaded rat room at night, but instead of rats, he discovered a hidden, tidy room full of books!

Tommy heard voices, and he quickly found a place to hide. It was Captain Stickybeard and his first mate, secretly studying about ancient treasures! They were finding big treasures for themselves and leaving silly little ones for the crew. But what made Tommy really angry was hearing them laugh at how they had tricked the crew into thinking that being uneducated was cool.

Fired up by this discovery, Tommy started secretly studying in the hidden room every night. He read about everything – from navigation to ancient civilizations. He learned so much and began to find smarter, faster ways to do things on the ship, though he pretended to be just a regular pirate.

Years passed, and Tommy became so knowledgeable that he could find treasure even before Captain Stickybeard. Finally, Tommy decided it was time to leave.

A week after he left, something amazing happened. For the first time, someone beat Captain Stickybeard to a treasure. Where the treasure should have been, Stickybeard found only a hollow skull with a big, mocking smile, surrounded by a pile of books. Of course, it was Tommy who found the treasure first, thanks to all the things he had learned!

That smiley skull became Clever Pirate Tom's symbol. With the treasure he found, Tom bought his own ship and gathered a crew of smart, educated sailors. Unlike Captain Stickybeard, Tom encouraged his crew to study and learn. Together, they found treasures much faster. Every time Captain Stickybeard arrived at a treasure site, all he found was a mocking skull.

Soon, all of Captain Stickybeard's crew left him to join Clever Pirate Tom, attracted by the promise of learning and fair sharing of treasures. And that's how Tommy went from a regular boy to the smartest pirate on the seven seas, showing everyone that knowledge is the greatest treasure of all.

Alex's Voyage into the Paper World

Once upon a time, there was a little boy named Alex who was very clever. His parents loved him. He was good at many things. He could draw, run really fast, and jump really high. He was good at math and at writing. He was full of great ideas. He only had one problem. He never finished anything.

If his teacher asked him to write about his weekend, he would get bored after writing about Friday night, and he would never get to Sunday. If he had to do a sum, he would do the first part, then something would distract him, and that was that. When his father told him to make his bed, he would place the pillow just perfectly, but he never got around to fixing the sheets or the blanket. It was a disaster.

Though Alex didn't know it, a magical creature from another world had been his protector since the day he was born. Half bear and half peacock, it was a curious little creature called Ariel, but Alex had never caught a glimpse of her.

Ariel knew things were going to go from bad to worse if Alex didn't learn to complete tasks. He had just never finished anything he wanted to do. So, Ariel told herself, "I have to teach him a lesson; he must go into the Paper World."

One morning, Alex excitedly drew a picture of his house and family. As usual, when the drawing was only half finished, he said, "I'm tired of drawing; that's good enough." But when he carelessly dropped his pencil, it sank into the drawing, disappearing into the paper. The same happened with everything else that touched the paper. The drawing grew larger, swallowing up the furniture and paintings in his room. Alex tried to stop it but found himself sinking into his drawing and becoming a part of it.

Inside this Paper World, Alex was in awe; what place was this, and how could he go back? As he took his first step, he tumbled over in pain. "Ouch!" he exclaimed. Beside him was his dog, Rover, who looked a bit odd with five legs and uncolored spots. "You didn't finish drawing yourself, Alex," Rover said, sounding almost human. Alex realized he had forgotten to draw one of his feet and now had to hop around.

When he tried to speak, Alex's words came out garbled. He had drawn only half his mouth. Examining himself, he found he was missing several fingers on his left hand, one of his elbows, and his nose. He even had a funny hairstyle. But Alex's biggest concern was for his parents. He wasn't sure if he had drawn their eyes and mouths.

He hopped around his half-drawn house, looking for his parents. But he had drawn them outside, and he couldn't go out because he hadn't drawn a door! As he pondered his next move, two horrible creatures began circling the house. They were monsters Alex had drawn when he was upset. They found their way in through an uncolored hole in the wall. "I should have colored this better," Alex thought, almost paralyzed with fear.

Rover, seeing the danger, urged Alex to follow him. "Piko can help us," he said. Alex was surprised. Piko was just a little songbird he had drawn. But in this paper world, Piko was huge!

They found Piko trapped in a tiny cage in the living room. Alex quickly freed the bird, and Piko lifted him and Rover into the air, helping them escape the monsters just in time. "Through the window, Piko!" Rover instructed. "Look, the monsters are in! "Through the window, Piko! We'll be safer outside."

Flying around the house, Alex spotted his pencil. He directed Piko to land near it. Once on the ground, he picked up the pencil and ran back to the house. He reached it just in time to fill in the uncolored spots on the wall, trapping the monsters inside.

"Good job!" Rover and Piko cheered. Alex, looking at his rushed work, took the pencil and began to correct his mistakes. But as he tried to draw with his incomplete arm, the pencil slipped, leaving a small black dot.

"Oh no!" Rover exclaimed. Piko asked, "What's wrong with a dot?" "It's not a dot; it's a black hole!" Rover replied.

The black hole grew rapidly, absorbing everything with unstoppable force. Suddenly, Alex found himself back at his table in the real world, his drawing complete. He noticed the fully colored wall in his drawing and sighed with relief. What a narrow escape!

Ariel, who had been watching everything from her hiding place, nodded with satisfaction. Alex had learned the importance of completing tasks. Ever since then, Alex always made sure to finish his drawings carefully, except for the monsters' feet – just in case.

Charlie and the Magical Inheritance

In a beautiful little town surrounded by rolling hills and lush woods, there lived an old man known far and wide for his remarkable work ethic and incredible skills. His name was Mr. Harrington, and he was a master craftsman who could fix anything. When he passed away, his belongings were divided among his three sons.

The eldest son, James, inherited Mr. Harrington's cozy, well-built house. The middle son, Peter, received the family's loyal cow, known for her plentiful milk. And the youngest, little Charlie, got his father's trusty axe and a sturdy pair of gloves.

James, settling into the house, spent his days relaxing, hardly bothering with upkeep. Peter, with the cow, started selling milk in the town market. But soon, he grew lazy, and the milk sales dwindled.

Meanwhile, Charlie, the youngest, put his heart into his work. With his father's axe and gloves, he helped neighbors chop wood, repaired broken fences, and even started

small construction projects. Over time, his reputation as a hardworking and skilled young man spread throughout the town.

Years passed, and the once beautiful house James inherited became dusty and shabby. Peter's cow, no longer cared for properly, stopped producing much milk. But Charlie, with his axe and gloves still in perfect condition, had built homes, bridges, and even a small dam. He had saved enough to buy his own house and a healthy, productive cow.

Seeing Charlie's success, James and Peter grew envious. They convinced themselves that Charlie's fortune must be due to some magic in the axe and gloves. One night, they quietly stole into Charlie's house and stole their brother's axe.

Excitedly, they tried to work with the axe, but nothing special happened.
Disappointed, they also stole the gloves, hoping for a change in their luck. Yet still, nothing happened.

Charlie, discovering his tools were gone, didn't get upset. Instead, he simply bought a new axe and gloves and continued his work with a cheerful heart, singing as he labored. His joy in his work was undiminished.

James and Peter finally realized the truth. Their father had left the greatest gift not in the house or the cow but in the lessons he had taught them – the value of hard work, perseverance, and a positive attitude. These qualities, not magical tools, were the secret to success.

Your Turn Now!

Dear brave explorer,

As we close the final pages of this wonderful journey, remember that the adventures you've read about are just the beginning. The stories in this book were not just tales of magic and daring deeds but also lessons that you can carry with you as you grow and explore the world around you.

You've met characters like Alex, who learned the importance of finishing what you start, and Tommy, who showed us how kindness can transform the world. You've sailed with Clever Pirate Tom, discovering that knowledge is the greatest treasure, and you've walked in the diligent footsteps of

Charlie, understanding that hard work and perseverance are keys to success.

Let these stories be like stars in the night sky, guiding you on your path. Keep them as reminders that within you lies the courage of a hero, the wisdom of a sage, and the heart of an adventurer. As you go forward in your own story, remember that you have the power to shape it, to overcome obstacles, and to reach for your dreams.

The end of this book is not the end of your adventure. It's just the beginning. You are the author of your own story, and every day is a blank page waiting for you to make your mark. Be bold, be curious, and be kind. Use the lessons from these stories to light your way, and never forget that you have the strength to make a difference.

So, dear boy, as you set this book down, know that your adventure continues. Dream big, believe in yourself, and step confidently into the world. The magic you've discovered here is just a glimpse of the magic that lies within you. Go forth and make your story one of courage, joy, and wonder.

Until we meet again in the pages of another book, keep the spirit of adventure alive in your heart.

Dear Parent who reads this book,

We hope you enjoyed the stories in it and the time spent discussing the valuable lessons they teach with your child.

For adults only ☺ we have prepared **a special guide that outlines 12 key concepts** with actionable ideas **to foster self-esteem and self-confidence in children**.

You can download, print, and put these ideas into practice regularly and integrate the proposed exercises into your child´s routine.

Get your guide here ↓

If you enjoyed this book, we encourage you to leave a review on its Amazon page so other parents can benefit from it as well

Made in the USA
Columbia, SC
09 December 2024

48909747R00048